About the Author

Johannes Viljoen was born in South Africa in 1965 and attended school at Grey College, Bloemfontein. Following school, he studied medicine at the University of Stellenbosch, South Africa, and qualified as a medical doctor in 1989. For the next decade or so, he practiced medicine in a variety of clinical disciplines, both in South Africa and the United Kingdom.

In 2003, he undertook a voyage by ship from Cape Town Harbour to the Island of Tristan da Cunha in the South Atlantic Ocean, where he was the medical officer for seven months. The island is known for being the most remote inhabited place on Earth, almost 3,000 kilometres from the shores of South Africa. At that time, there were 276 islanders living there. It was during his stay on this remotest island that he, on the good advice of his father, started to keep a journal with daily entries, and he continued to do so for many years since.

In 2005, he was accepted as a Fellow of the College of Pathologists (Medical Virology), through the Colleges of Medicine of South Africa.

In 2015, he obtained a PhD with distinction from the University of Montpellier in France. Founded in the 12th century, its Faculty of Medicine is the oldest in the world still in operation.

In *Jonny's on the Run...* he shares his notes taken between 2007 and 2009 at the Thunder Road Rock Diner on Florida Road, Durban, South Africa.

Jonny's on the Run...

Johannes Viljoen

Jonny's on the Run...

Illustrations by Celia van Niekerk

Olympia Publishers
London

www.olympiapublishers.com
OLYMPIA PAPERBACK EDITION

Copyright © Johannes Viljoen 2024

The right of Johannes Viljoen to be identified as author of
this work has been asserted in accordance with sections 77 and 78 of
the Copyright, Designs and Patents Act 1988.

All Rights Reserved

No reproduction, copy or transmission of this publication
may be made without written permission.
No paragraph of this publication may be reproduced,
copied or transmitted save with the written permission of the publisher,
or in accordance with the provisions
of the Copyright Act 1956 (as amended).

Any person who commits any unauthorised act in relation to
this publication may be liable to criminal
prosecution and civil claims for damage.

A CIP catalogue record for this title is
available from the British Library.

ISBN: 978-1-80439-543-1

This is a work of fiction.
Names, characters, places and incidents originate from the writer's
imagination. Any resemblance to actual persons, living or dead, is
purely coincidental.

First Published in 2024

Olympia Publishers
Tallis House
2 Tallis Street
London
EC4Y 0AB

Printed in Great Britain

Dedication

For Harry and friends.

CONTENTS

HARRY	11
CHARLIE THE VIKING	14
SPIDER TIME	17
MAGGIE THE WITCH	18
THE GRUDGE-MAKER	21
DUKE	23
THERE GOES A FOX	25
BRING ME THE BIGOT	26
HATCHET JOB IN A HATCHBACK	29
DEMONS	31
DUKE'S HANGOVER	32
I AM	34
MID-THIRTIES TO MID-FORTIES	35
IN THE QUIET OF DARKNESS	36
LITTLE WAYNE THE WAITER	37
OF LOVE	39
SALLY	40
FRIENDSHIP OF TIME	42
LITTLE WAYNE THE SMUGGLER	45
A LOVE LETTER	49
EXPAT-EDDIE	51
FOURTEEN WORDS ON A LONG RED STRING	53
EBOLA	56
DEATH OF AN UNKNOWN WOMAN	58
THE GOLFER	60
JONNY'S ON THE RUN	62
FISH	64

HARRY

The Frenchman and I were deep inside the sights and sounds of the night at the Thunder Road Rock Diner, opposite Hotel Benjamin on Florida Road. He always stayed at the Benjamin when visiting South Africa to work with me in my laboratory at the university in Durban. He said he loved staying there not only because he could smoke in his hotel room, but also because Thunder Road was right across the street from the hotel.

Just before the end of the band's second session, the Frenchman had managed, in broken English, to connect me to Harry whom he had met the night before in the bar. We were not going anywhere until the music was over, so I asked Harry if he had some *zol* to spare that would last us for the rest of the night. Harry was as decent as a stranger could be about such a request out of the blue, but with a few drags of his infamous homegrown 'Durban Poison', our fate at Thunder Road was sealed.

In the months following the Frenchman's last voyage and painful departure, Harry and I became good friends *(RIP Francois R, 'mon cher ami' – may we meet again)*. Harry is the kind of guy that would get up at night, grab his Colt .45, and come and help you if you were in a tight spot... he would, he did, and I will always love him for that.

So, it was not easy for me to respond when he complained that some people at Thunder Road who were friendly to him early in the evening, suddenly avoided him without reason later at night. Sure, he was pissed by that time, but in all fairness, so were almost everyone else in the bar, including the waiters.

I told him, "Harry, the people who know you well, are right to say that you are a damn fine bloke most of the time, especially from the beginning of the evening, just before your first pint to around your fifth one or so, then it sets in."

"What do you mean, then what sets in fucking where?" he countered defensively.

Personally, I have always maintained that it is a good thing not to know too much about anyone. Apart from being slightly deaf in the one ear and turning fifty, Harry was not in the habit of taking good advice from anyone, ever, and I suppose his stubbornness was starting to cost him now, more and more every day.

I said to Harry, "Well like, it's not as cool as you may think to tell acquaintances and other types of strangers that your mother had contact with beings from outer space. And that you not only saw the whole encounter first hand, you also remember it clear as day, even though you were only three years old when it happened. And listen here Harry, late at night in the bar, you tell this story to the same people twice per week, every week. That, is when they start to avoid you."

Harry was listening for a change, so I continued.

"Or like last Saturday night when you, in full view of everyone in the street, paid the car guard with a handful of bullets, instead of a handful of coins as always. He thought you were going to shoot him next, and so he spilled the bullets onto the road and vanished into the night like a ghost. You scared the hell out of him Harry, and me a little too. Fortunately, you two were equally wasted. You should give him a generous tip if he ever comes back here, dude."

Then I said to Harry, "And what about that cop car that passed us seconds later, with scattered bullets all shiny in the road, and you sitting drunk behind the wheel of your pick-up truck? If they bust you, pray they are inner city cops and not real ones. Likely you will need at least five hundred rand just to get them to listen to your side of the story. But it will be more like two thousand rand in cash in the end, all depending on how rich, and how wasted, you appear to them. Focus on the guy who seems to be in charge. Most likely he is the one initially hanging back in the shadows, observing you at first, to see how "bribe-able" you may be, and vice versa.

Then, after his deputies have worked you over a little bit and started falling back one by one, he will call you over for a more private conversation, away from the group. If you see some gold in his teeth, it could be a very good sign, but not always, so you have to be careful Harry. Don't overplay your hand, and don't thank your lucky stars too quickly. Things can change fast."

"However, if you can't pay up, they will lock you up in the holding cells till Monday, then it's game over for you old chap. From what I heard, it will be a Sunday that you will never forget, mister! And stop looking at me like that, I don't even own a gun. But you are right, nothing bad happened, and yes, it was actually quite funny and ridiculous at the same time!" We both laughed. Harry lit a last one, and we headed back to the music.

I feel for Harry, especially late at night when he starts lecturing people, knowing more about everything and anything than anyone, anywhere, into eternity. Harry has a big heart and a big gun in his pickup truck. He is also convinced that he is immensely wise and can 'see into people'.

But to be fair, standing up, he is neither very tall nor very wide and remains both the leading and mostly the only character in his self-composed never-ending short story, entitled *"Harry... often in love, always at war."*

CHARLIE THE VIKING

We called him 'Charlie the Viking', because he spoke and laughed and drank like we thought a Viking should, and he was huge and had blue Viking eyes that became vicious quickly, even though he was already grey and sixty-four. All he would ever admit to about himself, was that he was originally from Denmark, and in the 'shipping business'. He now has a home in the Philippines somewhere, where he often goes to, his Nordic past way behind him.

Charlie was a new face at Thunder Road, and Harry and I liked talking to him. We knew he wouldn't stay long; his sort never did. I gave him a week or so, Harry said two. Whenever he wanted to speak, he would raise his big right hand index finger and say, *"Now Listen to Me!"*, and we would all keep quiet immediately, listening like our lives depended on it.

Charlie had shipping tattoos with a military flavour. Charlie said the past is the past, and it did not bother him anymore, and that death would always look ugly in his line of work.

One afternoon Charlie was sitting at an outside table in the sun at Thunder Road and called me over for a drink. He had just finished reading an investigative book on international crime syndicates and said that I can have it, and that it will answer many of the questions that Harry and I have been asking him the whole week. I asked Charlie to write a message in the front. He wrote my name, his name, and the words *"read this, son."* Harry joined us a bit later and spoke to Charlie about his recurring nightmare where he is running frenzied and feverishly, hacking his way through thorn bushes while bleeding, with a ferocious pack of Viking wolves at his heels. And did Charlie think it was his past, or maybe his future, that he was dreaming of?

Charlie said that once you become an opium eater, you discover the little heaven inside hell, and then nothing will ever be the same for you again. And in between you, your little heaven inside your fiery hell, and the real heaven, is just an empty space with your name on it, and that, he said, is the only place left you can build on.

"Build what, Charlie?" I asked.

"Your rock," he said. "The one you must stand on if you want to fight for your life. Or you can of course decide not to fight, and thereby not to live, and go here or there when it is all over."

"But for Vikings, entrance into Valhalla is denied if you had lived a coward's life," Charlie added as an afterthought.

Later I said to Harry that we were going to miss Charlie, and that it's really cool to live in a port city where you get to meet Vikings, and other knowledgeable people in the 'shipping business.' Harry chuckled at that, which was unusual for him.

SPIDER TIME

Little spider in your cosy spot,
can you see the future?
Can you see it not?

Little spider in a cuckoo clock,
time spins under key,
time spins under lock.

Little spider not yet beaten,
father time,
has not yet eaten.

Little spider holds his breath,
four times in sixty,
near his death.

Little spider has not heard,
you do not fear,
a wooden bird.

MAGGIE THE WITCH

Harry and I were drinking at Thunder Road when Maggie turned up… Maggie the Witch. She was like a loaded gun. Harry pointed her in everyone's direction, and everyone ducked. Maggie cackled her loud witch's cackle.

Maggie sold pork meat to butchers and restaurants in the Durban area that came from her brother's pig farm in the mountains. He also has chickens, and that's where Maggie learned how to negotiate life, pecking around like a blind chicken, hopefully to find food with a lucky strike.

She slammed down a twenty rand note on the table in the spilled wine, because I had bought her a drink earlier on my tab. I left it lying on the table for a while in the spilled wine. Maggie didn't have a lot of money, and she kept on eyeing it just in case the breeze would blow it off the table. She asked me about twenty times if I had taken it, and I said yes, it is mine, I am just letting it lie there for a while. I said she could take it back if she wanted to, but she refused, saying, *"I Pay my Own Way!"*, cackling her loudest witch's cackle of the night. Then she became dismally rude, as all defeated witches eventually do, and turned her back on me to talk to a Chinese man. So I paid with my credit card and tore up the soaked twenty rand note into twenty pieces and left it lying on the table in the breeze and the spilled wine. Harry said it was like paying a car guard with bullets, and I had to agree, and left.

I would have given anything to see her face when she saw her twenty rand note, which was now mine, torn up into twenty pieces in the wine. But I never did, and I never will. Harry saw, but he won't be able to tell me either. It is just one of those things you have to see for yourself.

Her expression would not have been the same had I still been there in any case.

THE GRUDGE-MAKER

You strike me as someone who prefers –
no, indeed, loves – to bear a grudge,
and to bear it bravely and with much care,
and that it is your habit to secretly hide away
a multitude of collections of this poison,
to hide it away deep within the caverns of your soul,

in such a manner and so carefully constructed,
that there is an insidious seepage of this poison,
the nature of which in fact serves to feed your thirsty soul,
and your greedy mind and the remains of your heart,
and by its nature, the grudge itself,
so that it may continue to produce its deadly poison.

So allow me, the grudge-maker,
to present and give to you a grudge to bear forever inside,
and with you for eternity, and that you will not be rid of,
while present here with us, the living,
and for which none of any efforts on your part,
will even remotely remedy your condition.

DUKE

Harry had this friend called Duke who always introduced himself at Thunder Road with "Hi, I am Duke, and I'm on lithium. My doctor put me on it because I'm completely crazy!" And then he would laugh loudly, but always alone. We didn't mind at all having Duke around, whichever cards life had dealt him for the day. And we all knew that Duke wasn't crazy at all. His doctor, however, insisted that he suffers from what is known as a 'cyclothymic' personality disorder.

"What the fuck does that even mean?" Harry asked me later when we were alone.

I replied, "Well, Harry, in layman's terms, it means that Duke is sometimes overly exuberant and at other times extremely blue, but hanging mostly on Mondays, in between planet Mars and the Moon."

Harry grinned, "I understand exactly what you mean, 'doc', and on top of it all, it sounds like almost everyone I know."

Duke made a life out of spearfishing barracuda and yellow fin tuna in the Indian Ocean. He also gave surfing lessons for beginners and played the bass guitar in a rock and roll band. He even had a girlfriend whose name was Charm, and of all the girls around, she had by far the most tattoos, and I guess she was, well, charming in a sort of colourful way. Someone once said she was a stripper, but that Duke did not mind, just as long as no one touched her. Whenever I spoke to her, she always had this beautiful, warm smile.

I will never forget the first time I met Duke. He's got this gap in between his front teeth, but in a good-looking way, like a famous actor or something. So, the first time we started chatting I asked him where his family was from, and what they did, and he said, "My father is a 'useless priest'." Just like that, and I will never forget the way he said it. It came out really sad, with pain in his eyes, and not mean at all as he had tried to say it. When I asked him why, he said, "Because he can't fix me!"

I did not understand what Duke meant at the time, but afterwards Harry told me that his mother and father were very strict and devoted religious leaders in their church. Duke had been excommunicated three times now because of what he did, and what he said, and why he came to the pub, hanging out with people like us, and all that.

"Where does he live?" I asked Harry.

"In a cottage in the back of his parents' place north of Durban," Harry said, staring into his warm beer.

THERE GOES A FOX

I play the violin,
but always carry
a knife.

I cry on women's shoulders,
but always have
a wife.

I tangle with snakes,
but dilute their poison
with life.

BRING ME THE BIGOT

So…
you know what it's like,
the bigots hate the bigots,
accusing each other of bigotry,
and through their bigotry,
they murder the argument
instead of cynicism's evil little twin,
the bigotry.

So…
gouge out the eyes of the bigots, I say.
Pour wisdom into the empty sockets,
like molten copper,
onto the raw flesh
of those bigots,
making themselves guilty
of bloody bigotry.

HATCHET JOB IN A HATCHBACK

We were drinking at Thunder Road and Harry was talking crazy shit through his beard and going on and on about something as guys who smoked *zol* every day, which he does, do. Just then these two girls walked in, one very short and one very tall. "Aye... will you look at these two slappers." As only Harry could creep. They each had a shooter and a cocktail of some sort and sat at a table nearby. They were nice.

"The short one has a pretty face," I said, "and a nice laugh too."

"Well, I like the tall one's ass," Harry creeped again. We got another round. Harry was staring at them, but they didn't look back. "If the short one's head were on the tall one's body, she'd be the best-looking chick in the pub," Harry grunted in a creepy way, within earshot this time.

"I could always cut the short one's head off with my knife in the back of your hatchback and put it on the tall one's body," he said, and then thought of something, grinning into his beard.

So, we popped out leaving the broads to the lucky fellas in the bar, and while walking up to the café to get some cigarettes, this drunk couple was having a 'helluva fight' right in front of us. Suddenly the guy turned and put his fist through a thick shop window right up to his elbow. She went ballistic, and someone else was screaming in the background that it was her brother and that they were from Johannesburg.

"And...?" Harry said to that. She was in shock.

The drunk guy was a stocky son-of-a-bitch and by the time

we got there his girl had taken her top off to try and stop the bleeding, and only had a pinkish bra on.

She was beautiful, and pissed as well, and hysterical with blood pouring from his arm, lots of blood. I stared at her breasts, and she stared at the wound, crying into the blood. People were starting to gather, and a police car arrived.

Harry proclaimed loudly and proudly that I was a doctor, and everyone turned and started screaming at me. I said to hold him still so that I could have a look. It was really messed up. Fortunately the cuts missed the artery, but not the tendons or the big veins of the upper arm. I said to keep up the pressure and to wait for an ambulance, and that there was nothing more that I could do.

I looked at the blood spurting onto her breasts. She was so sexy, but the drunk guy was a real nutcase and started giving me all sorts of verbal shit. He must have seen me staring at his girlfriend with lust, instead of staring at his wound with concern, like any good Samaritan passing by should. He was clearly of the jealous type, even though he was right about it.

However, at that stage of the game, he was not in a very commanding position to bargain with the good doctor, from.

As I started walking away, his girlfriend yelled at me that I was a useless cunt of a doctor, and by then she had a nipple stand; she couldn't have been more than twenty-four, beautiful pink nipples, erect with blood on.

"Fuck! Did you see him bleed?" Harry said. Not as much as a hatchet job in a hatchback with your blunt knife would, I thought.

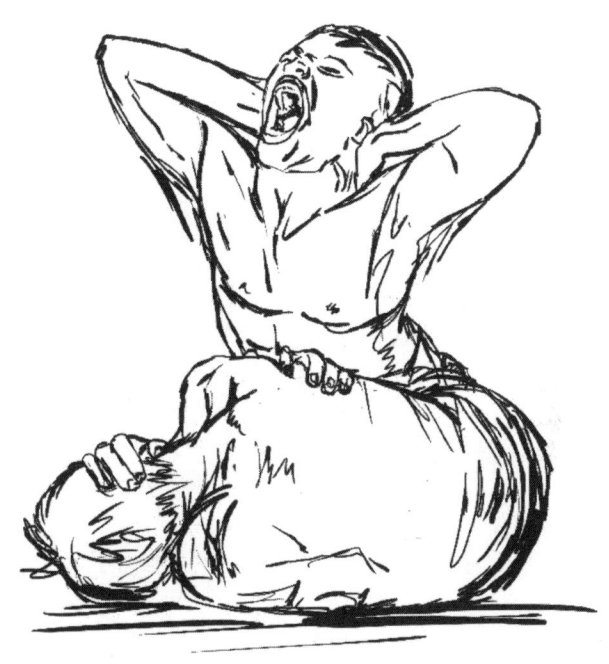

DEMONS

(Chorus crescendo)

Let us bend him over backwards
and tie him in a knot!
Then send him off into the world
and see if he can straighten up!

DUKE'S HANGOVER

Duke felt like he was going to get run over by a car at any moment, even standing right in the middle of a park. He just couldn't shake the feeling. He had it when he woke up, even checked for cars as he got out of bed. No more late nights in the week, he swore, not with that lot!

Maggie came running down the hill hollering her witch's holler. "Duke! Duke! Did you hear what happened to Jonny and Harry at Thunder Road last night?"

Maggie's voice sliced through Duke's demented mind like a knife through lava. How does she keep it up? he wondered. She was with them the night before, and one of the last ones to leave the bar. She probably has a witch's brew at home that makes her immune to these things. The thought of it made him want to be sick, but by the time Maggie had finally finished her hollering-while-running-down-the-hill, the feeling was gone.

"You, okay?" she asked. Duke nodded, stuck a cigarette in his mouth and pointed to her to sit on the bench. Maggie was telling the story so fast, cackling so loudly, that Duke had to hold his hand up against her face, her mind, and her tongue. Somewhere in the background, screeching tyres smashed into something.

Harry and I saw Duke later that night, but he couldn't remember Maggie's story. We told him that several things had happened to both of us last night. Maybe we couldn't remember either.

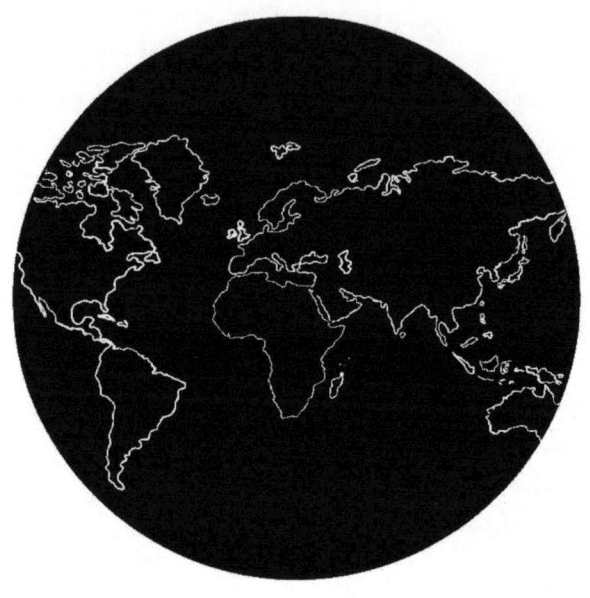

I AM

I am evolution;
I am a citizen of the world.
I am bound by my country,
but not by my soul.

MID-THIRTIES TO MID-FORTIES

Duke was miserable so Harry told him it was his own fault, and that everyone knows you should never look too deep into the soul of a dying woman, at least not up close like he did.

Especially if she had dark eyes, was beautiful and lonely as well. Duke said she told him how good it was to see him again, and that he has a fascinating mind. But nothing would ever come of it because he was far too nervous and talked too much, and that if she had to live with him again, she would eventually kill him.

We could see Duke knew she meant it. This time his eyes didn't lie.

IN THE QUIET OF DARKNESS

He knew! But how so, they disagreed on.
'It's from living there,' said one, 'so very long!'
'No! It's from what happened there,' said some, 'and is gone',
and much is spoken for, and finally agreed upon.

How fearful it is to behold the sight,
of one that ventures beyond the limits of light,
on a lonesome dance, on a lonesome night,
with soul intact, indeed, the colour of white.

With a heart so gentle, a mind so clear,
whom mad and sane alike desire to hear,
can it be true, can it be near?
The path there and back, and never a tear.

LITTLE WAYNE THE WAITER

Little Wayne was telling the story to Big Wayne, although they were approximately the same size. Harry and I and almost everyone else at Thunder Road knew that Little Wayne was not supposed to drink while serving customers, especially not taking small sips from customers' drinks, even if they were so full, they were going to spill a little in the tray 'anyway.' So, we never bought him any drinks while he was on duty so that he would not get fired, even though he sometimes tried to sell us drugs.

He was telling Big Wayne the big story of how Thunder Road was shut down by the police on Saturday night because of the band's noise, but he mostly remembered what happened to him just before that. He said the place was so packed, and that people were crammed in so tight, pointing to a small concrete block on the sidewalk to show that two persons had to stand on the same sidewalk slab.

He told us how he used to go to a place called "Burn", called that because it had previously burnt down, where people really had to shove each other properly to get a drink. And here he was standing in a relatively well-behaved crowd all pushing each other softly-softly for a drink. He said softly twice and demonstrated by making soft forward pushing moves with his arms, while standing on the slab with another imaginary person next to him. And how while serving a table he considered giving the person next to him a good shove to see if he would then shove the next person to him, and so on until everyone was shoving each other properly, like at Burn.

But he stopped short with his hands in the air because just then the police arrived due to the noise, and not because of any proper shoving, and at least no one was caught smoking cigarettes inside, due to the type of licence they had.

He said you get all sorts of different licences, like for restaurants, bars, night clubs, strip clubs etc… and the more you paid, the more you could do.

OF LOVE

Why should I be scared?
It is a simple thing.
You cannot force love.
Love will force you.
If I create the space,
Will you colour it in?

SALLY

Sally bought me a drink at Thunder Road the other day, even though she was low on cash. By now she was HIV positive as well, just as everybody had warned her of her deadly habits. Her parents told her that God was punishing her for her character, and for refusing to be like her sister, brother, and idiot-cousin, she said.

But long before God had punished her with HIV, he punished her with all sorts of other things, always making an example of her. I replied that HIV was a disease, and not a punishment, but rather a consequence, and that we were surrounded by millions of other people also infected. She could go onto a government programme with free treatment and drugs, which could buy her many years of good health, that she could even still have children.

But her only response was that she knew exactly what and when it had happened, and it was all because she had a bush between her legs instead of a Brazilian cut which is common these days. Her bush drove this guy crazy with lust and desire. He told her that cut, if not shaved regularly, felt like stubble, reminding him of a man's beard when he went down on his woman.

Sally had this sexy gap between her front teeth, like a famous singer, and the men who liked her for her bush, liked her for that as well.

FRIENDSHIP OF TIME

So let us all stand together,
and drink a toast of wine forever,
for indeed, splendid sirs of time,
your health, appears to be mine.

So to my friend of dogs and mercy
to my heart and mind you are worthy
and to my friend of honour and mime
ours truly withstood the test of time.

So let us all stand forever,
and drink a toast of wine together,
and wink and fight life, my brother,
as well as, of course, each other.

LITTLE WAYNE THE SMUGGLER

Harry and I were chatting to Little Wayne, the friendly ex-waiter at Thunder Road. Little Wayne said that coincidentally, he does not believe in coincidence, and that's why he quit his job as a waiter at Thunder Road and was now selling illegal cigarettes. He only did three or maybe four runs a month from some of the ships in the harbour. That kept him sharp and minimised his risk of getting busted, while still having enough money to live on for the rest of the month, selling his merchandise to his clients.

Little Wayne added that, in his opinion as an ex-waiter, it was very easy to run a rock bar. None of this made any sense to Harry and they got into an argument about why running a rock bar like Thunder Road was not just about picking up empty glasses, which was the easy part, but what if workers didn't pitch and the ice was late, and the place was pumping? "So-what-would-you-do? What-would-you-do?" Harry shouted at Little Wayne who first had to ponder the scenario and then said politely:

"No, but then it's the managers problem." Pointing to them inside the bar. We realised that this conversation was not going anywhere, and we both stared at Little Wayne in silence.

Then Little Wayne said that the reason why his elderly clients liked him was not only because of this or that, but also because he could spot a murderer a mile away, not that he was particularly strong or armed or anything. It was just that he knew better than anyone who were the troublemakers, and who were safe, and that's what they admired in him.

I later said to Harry that Little Wayne was probably the ideal candidate for low key illegal cigarette distribution, especially in a port city, and he conceded.

A LOVE LETTER

Thoughts of you, sane and insane,
rage blood red through my heart;
tell me you understand.
whisper 'yes' in my ear.

I feel ill in your shadow.
You see right through me;
you devour me and spit out
what you do not want.

Let the dead memories die.
Drive them from my soul.
Bring forth my hidden desire,
my love for you is unbowed.

Embrace me! But do so quickly
for I am swept down a river;
there will drown your lover,
there a sad friend remains.

EXPAT-EDDIE

Harry and I were at Thunder Road when expat-Eddie, who now lives in London, said what a brilliant decision it was to leave South Africa and go and live in the UK, as he had done. And that he couldn't understand why everyone else was not joining him in his spectacular move.

Expat-Eddie said that one of the perks of living in London was that he ate and drank very well over there. I said that surely we also have good food and wine in South Africa, but that was not what he wanted to hear, or came to Thunder Road for, on that particular night.

He said another first world perk was that if you buy a 1st class postage stamp for 85 p to send a letter to anyone anywhere in the UK, you are guaranteed that it would reach its destination the next day. But he couldn't recall ever mailing a letter to anyone anywhere in the country, who then received it the next day.

I pointed out to expat-Eddie that while some people live by calculation only, like him, others, like Harry, mainly live by instinct as well. I said to him that he was always calculating risks and rewards between good and not so good options, like life moves, choosing a woman, a job, a country, and so on. And if it looks okay on paper, then it ought to be okay in real life also. But everyone knows it never is.

Whereas compared to that, Harry mostly let 'opportunities' beyond his control happen first, before then setting sail to act upon it. It is the more risky path, but comes with music. That's also why it was so important for expat-Eddie to know how he compared to others, because their assessments of him would somehow be the most accurate method available to measure his own success by, and worth its weight in gold. As long as he stayed ahead of the pack.

But expat-Eddie carried on with his self-justification, each step calculatingly mapped out. I tried to imagine myself in expat-Eddie's mind, but it was claustrophobic and drowning in doubt. I think he likes me because I have truly accepted him for what he is, and I, in turn, tolerated him because I realised that it was essential for him to surround himself with people whom it was easy to be better-than, even if only in his eyes.

Expat-Eddie was desperate for me to acknowledge that he had done the right thing to emigrate, rather than stay in South Africa. But I didn't, I couldn't, and that made him drink a bit more, and a bit louder than usual that night. I reassured him that he is a very talented bloke, who would be fine wherever he went and that if he stuck to his plan, he may even enter politics as a conservative party member as he had always dreamt about. He liked that bit of my story.

Later that night he said that he wants me to know that he was doing his best to be a good ambassador for 'us' in the UK, even though we both knew he didn't really give a fuck about anyone not 'us'. And that regardless of all the variables, he would forever be a prisoner of his own ego, living alone high up in the cold of his ivory tower.

I tried to leave expat-Eddie with an inspiring thought, but realised that any form of inspiration would likely be lost on him. So, I opened my mouth just to close it again, and left.

FOURTEEN WORDS ON A LONG RED STRING

Doctor Dirk the dentist was getting drunk in a bad way with his new girlfriend at Thunder Road after his band, tired of his bullshit, had finally kicked him out. Just as Harry, Duke, and even Maggie had predicted barely two weeks ago after he had the band's name tattooed on his forearm. Doctor Dirk was busy trying to convince anyone who would care to listen, of the 'power of words'.

To prove his point, he told us about the time he was arrested at a biker bar on the other side of the city for his involvement in a brawl with three bikers that went horribly wrong. "Not that brawls can go right actually," he added dryly.

In the chaos that ensued, one of the bikers got badly injured and had to go to hospital for treatment. Doctor Dirk said it was not his fault, never was and never will be. They attacked him first, from behind, and there was a witness, a guy he was talking to, somewhere in the background, somewhere in the shadows, who would be able to confirm his version of events, if only he could find him again.

But instead of a friend or a witness, it was a detective and his deputy that knocked on Doctor Dirk's front door the next morning. The detective shook his head at Doctor Dirk's feeble attempts to explain himself, and advised him not to say anything further, but to rather get a good criminal lawyer, as he was going to need one. He went on to say that, in his opinion, Doctor Dirk's response to the attack was excessive and unjustified even though he did not start the fight, and then proceeded to arrest him right there in the kitchen on a charge of attempted murder, reading him his rights with the gardener and the house-keeper's son looking on in silence.

On the way to the police station in the back of the police car, the detective asked him wryly, "So how does someone who is a doctor end up getting tattoos?"

Doctor Dirk blinked twice and replied, "You should rather ask how does someone with tattoos, get to be a doctor." And that was all it took to change Doctor Dirk's destiny… fourteen words on a long red string.

Doctor Dirk saw the detective looking pensively out the car window, as if Doctor Dirk's words had reminded him of someone or somewhere from long ago, but in a special way. Halfway to the station and without saying a word, the deputy removed Doctor Dirk's handcuffs, saying with his eyes only that they do not regard him as dangerous or a flight risk, but that they would 'fuck-him-up' properly in the event that he did try something. While taking Doctor Dirk's fingerprints at the station, the detective said to him that he had decided to reduce the charges against him from attempted murder to involuntary assault, which was still serious, but a whole lot better.

Wiping away small drunken tears Doctor Dirk told us that when he appeared in court to plead that afternoon, he was shackled in chains around his ankles and tied to five other men already in the holding cell. The six of them were then shuffled up the stairs into the court room in a straight 'not-guilty-line', of which he was last. But the worst part of this whole episode, he cried, was that he was forced to sell his own limited edition motorcycle that only comes in black, to pay back his debt, and that tore up his heart into a thousand broken words on a long black string.

Doctor Dirk's case was eventually settled out of court some months later and all charges against him, paid for in full with borrowed money, were dropped, and the system kicked him out, a free man once more.

EBOLA

My name is Simon, and it is Monday here in Sierra Leone. It has been five days, and no one has shown any beads of sweat on their foreheads, not even the three little ones we keep away from everyone in the back room. Sometimes in the middle of the day it is hot, and you don't know why you are sweating, but you are farming in the sun, for food, so is it normal?

But then it goes away when you rest in the shade, and then you can relax, and think. I watch everyone every day. All thirty-five of us remaining in the small village now. Even myself. I watch myself every day, but especially visitors, which is the worst. How do you watch them, how do you know?

It has been twelve days since the last death, and he was the one who went to the other village for food, for us. He brought back the Ebola with him. We burnt his body last night right where it lay in the street. It was the smell that upset the children and the women, more than the fear of Ebola that made us burn it in the end.

The people are striking, "We cannot go on any more. Forget the dead! We want more money, but most of all, we want to sleep! We don't want to pick up dead bodies in these sweaty suits any more!"

We kept our distance from him when the fever took him. We took petrol from the small broken motorbike and, to save ourselves first, we burnt him, as they had told us. We had to do it, he was our uncle, and he went for food, it was our responsibility. And now we wait. We wait, and we watch, every day.

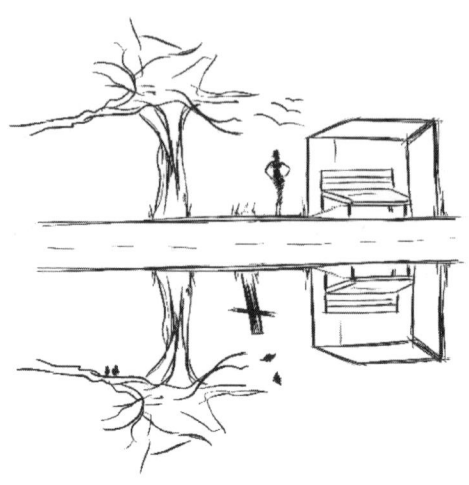

DEATH OF AN UNKNOWN WOMAN

This morning, in my street, I saw your small white cross in the sunshine under the trees and the birds. A small bunch of flowers now dried up, blown away by the wind, into the dust from whence it came. The only memory of you now is a small white wooden cross, that will soon be gone as well, forever. The newspaper said you were an unknown woman, late twenties to early thirties, that you had been murdered the night before, and that people had seen you at the bus stop for a few nights recently, waiting for your man, and his money, so that you could enter oblivion, happy once more, once for a while.

Did you come from inland somewhere, dead one? Did those who called you here say it would be easier to work under the warm Durban night sky, that it would be better for you to avoid the harsh winters, scattered somewhere inland? Did you look in their eyes, did you believe them, and – most preciously – was a new hope born that finally turned your direction around?

Their promises, or their promises of lies! Did they say that once here, fate would relent on her unbridled lashing of you—a woman of the night? No! And did they convince you that all malice would miraculously be withdrawn from your so-desperate journey through life, if only you would listen? No, once more! But still you came.

Who now will bring your mother tidings of her daughter's death? Is your mother still alive, will she cry for you, daughter? Or are you the one we should call "dead mother"? Are your children still alive, will they cry for you, mother? And yet you came, all the while unaware that an unseen horror from the depths of hell had arisen to cross paths with you? And that your end was to be a brutal, violent, bloody death in the darkness of night under the trees and the bats across from the bus stop.

The 'demon,' because surely it can only be a demon and his servant, manifesting as a grunting, sex-preying monster who – dare I even say it! – savagely mutilated your femininity with a broken bottle, and that you were strangled as well, but by God I pray, in what sequence?

Did you not feel death's presence drawing near that night, while you were waiting on your own at the bus stop? Is that how it started, silently and innocently, dead one?

Or were you perhaps thrilled to be in the company of a magnificently diabolical companion, death's accomplice, enjoying cheap wine and drunk with laughter, wildly gesticulating you did not hear the Reaper approach? By the time you saw the flames of madness dancing in the eyes of your possessed companion, it was already too late for you not to die, and everything had already become irrevocably insane.

Before a little white cross appeared one day under a tree in my street, I did not know of your existence. You were just another unknown woman, from a distant land, now murdered and forgotten. I cried for you the other night, but I was drunk. May you rest in peace. I will always remember your beautiful little spot under the trees, in the sunshine and with the birds.

THE GOLFER

I died suddenly and without too much fuss, just in time to see my birdie putt fall on the thirteenth green. It was a great put. Ironically, this only days after telling everyone that I have never felt better before. The thirteenth hole has been good to me over the years and one of my favourites. The pain was sharp but quickly forgotten and started somewhere in the upper parts of my being and stopped abruptly behind my left eye, then slowly drifted down to the middle of my chest.

    Initially I could not hear what they were saying but heard the cart approaching through the trees and their voices slowly became audible through the mist. I always suspected that the back seat of a golfing cart would not hold an entire body in prone position. My left leg kept on dangling off the one side because the handlebar was broken. Pierre kept on pulling it back up with his putter to prevent it from scraping on the ground. His face was white, and I saw a speck of a tear in his one eye, but maybe it was the wind. One of the spikes on my shoe was missing and I swear that's why I hooked my drive on the previous tee.

The journey to Mombasa was naturally cancelled and instead most of the group gathered for a small and stuffy occasion to celebrate my cremation in a small village on the west coast. Why on earth I chose this venue, no one would ever know now. Not even old Uncle Ignatius in the mountains could recall that I had ever mentioned the place, never mind visited it, although Ann said the telephone connection was poor and that she was not sure if it was the line or Uncle Ignatius's voice that was crackling so much. We were close. She refused to accept the container with my ashes and waved it away despite her brother's insistence. She had always maintained that she would never be sure it was mine, and I knew she would later burn a few photographs and some of my more meaningful belongings and scatter it in private in the waves from our rock by the sea, as we had murmured and agreed late one night, long ago.

It is strange and quite beautiful to see from here your tears that are a soft satin fragmented colour of purple when you remember me, and how it changes to black red when you become angry.

JONNY'S ON THE RUN

"Jonny's on the run…" said Harry to Duke because they had not seen him for a while. So, Duke asked Harry from what? Harry said that apparently he was not running away from anything, but rather towards something that's got to do with dreams and nightmares and that kind of stuff.

"Well, how long has he been running, and did he find it?" asked Duke.

"He's been running for forty-four years, and he did find stuff, but only stuff that made him run faster, and further away," Harry replied.

"Shit, I hope he gets what he wants before he is too 'dog-gone-tired' 'so-to-speak'," a Chinese man blurted out from the next table.

Duke replied worryingly, "He should be careful, he seems to be running around in circles, and soon to a standstill he will come. And what if he hates the place where he ends up? What if there is no fish to eat at the end of the road?"

"What if the end of the road is in China?" said the Chinese man with a twinkle in his eyes.

That night everyone had nightmares of fish breaking all the rules by running themselves to standstill in underwater circles of blackness.

FISH

And late at night, when I have stopped running and am finally and thankfully alone, I think of all the friendly faces I meet in books, and on blogs, and in bars… and then I eat fish, all kinds of fish. Raw fish like rollmops and herring, and tinned fish like tuna and sardines, and fresh ocean fish, of which there is a wide variety.

I should live a long time, if you can believe all you hear in books, and on blogs, and in bars. Then I dream strange, beautiful dreams of fish swimming into the future in purple, blue, and silver underwater circles of tranquillity.

FIN